Joseph-Alexandre de Chabrier de Peloubet

Family Records of Joseph Alexander de Chabrier de Peloubet

The first of the name in the United States with the funeral address of his

eldest son L. M. F. Chabrier Peloubet who died Nov. 28, 1885

Joseph-Alexandre de Chabrier de Peloubet

Family Records of Joseph Alexander de Chabrier de Peloubet
The first of the name in the United States with the funeral address of his eldest son
L. M. F. Chabrier Peloubet who died Nov. 28, 1885

ISBN/EAN: 9783337424510

Printed in Europe, USA, Canada, Australia, Japan

Cover: Foto ©Raphael Reischuk / pixelio.de

More available books at **www.hansebooks.com**

OF

Joseph Alexander de Chabrier de Peloubet

THE FIRST OF THE NAME IN THE UNITED STATES

WITH

THE FUNERAL ADDRESS OF HIS ELDEST SON

L. M. F. Chabrier Peloubet

𝕎ho died 𝕹ov. 28, 1885

————————

1892

PRINTED FOR THE FAMILY

COAT OF ARMS
OF THE DESCHWEILER OF DE TUFFR

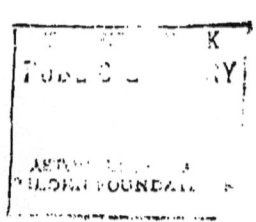

CHATEAU DE FELOUBET,

EAST FRONT

CHATEAU DE PELOUBET
NORTH FRONT

CHATEAU DE PELOUBET.
SOUTH FRONT

32

4—60

64— i.

3—52

68— i.
67— ii.

3—53

70— i.

4—70

3—54

—136 Olive Cl...

8—131 Charlott...
1875.

140— i. Herbert C...
141— ii. Prescott ...

3—132 Annie W...

144— i. William ...

—X. Descendau...
McCoy,
1865.

le

LEMAN, 1875.

160— iii. Gr